Hurricane Rescue

Written by
Rekha S. Rajan

Illustrated by
Courtney Lovett

SCHOLASTIC INC.

For all the communities and families who have been impacted by
hurricanes and those who came to help. —RSR

For my family, who lend a helping hand
through the worst storms. —CL

During any disaster, please make sure to follow instructions from trusted adults.

If you purchased this book without a cover, you should be aware that this book is stolen property. It was reported as "unsold and destroyed" to the publisher, and neither the author nor the publisher has received any payment for this "stripped book."

Text copyright © 2024 by Rekha S. Rajan
Illustrations © 2024 by Courtney Lovett

All rights reserved. Published by Scholastic Inc., *Publishers since 1920*. SCHOLASTIC, BRANCHES, and associated logos are trademarks and/or registered trademarks of Scholastic Inc.
DISASTER SQUAD is a registered trademark of Rekha S. Rajan.

The publisher does not have any control over and does not assume any responsibility for author or third-party websites or their content.

No part of this publication may be reproduced, stored in a retrieval system, or transmitted in any form or by any means, electronic, mechanical, photocopying, recording, or otherwise, without written permission of the publisher. For information regarding permission, write to Scholastic Inc., Attention: Permissions Department, 557 Broadway, New York, NY 10012.

This book is a work of fiction. Names, characters, places, and incidents are either the product of the author's imagination or are used fictitiously, and any resemblance to actual persons, living or dead, business establishments, events, or locales is entirely coincidental.

Library of Congress Cataloging-in-Publication Data

Names: Rajan, Rekha S., author. | Lovett, Courtney, illustrator. Title: Hurricane rescue / written by Rekha S. Rajan ; illustrated by Courtney Lovett. Description: First edition. | New York : Branches/Scholastic, 2024. | Series: Disaster squad ; 2 | Audience: Ages 7–10. | Audience: Grades 2–3. | Summary: The Jackson family travels to Texas, where a hurricane is heading down the coast, and there are animals, wildlife, and people in danger—but first, they have to ride out the storm at a local shelter.

Identifiers: LCCN 2023032993 | ISBN 9781338828863 (paperback) |
ISBN 9781338828870 (hardback) | ISBN 9781338828887 (ebook)
Subjects: LCSH: Hurricanes—Juvenile fiction. | Animal rescue—Juvenile fiction. | Natural disasters—Juvenile fiction. | Families—Juvenile fiction. | Texas—Juvenile fiction. | CYAC: Hurricanes—Fiction. | Animal rescue—Fiction. | Natural disasters—Fiction. | Family life—Fiction. | Texas—Fiction. Classification: LCC PZ7.1.R3456 Hu 2024 | DDC 813.6 [Fic] —dc23/eng/20230801 LC record available at https://lccn.loc.gov/2023032993

ISBN 978-1-338-82887-0 (hardcover) / ISBN 978-1-338-82886-3 (paperback)

10 9 8 7 6 5 4 3 2 1   24 25 26 27 28

Printed in India
First edition, October 2024
Illustrated by Courtney Lovett
Edited by Katie Heit
Book design by Jaime Lucero

Table of Contents

1. Welcome to Texas 1
2. Flat Tire 8
3. Rattlesnake! 11
4. Hurricane Season 16
5. Tabby Cat 22
6. Community Shelter 28
7. Dos and Don'ts 36
8. Hurricane Connor 40
9. Shadow Puppet Show 45
10. Flood! 50
11. Board Up 56
12. Hail! 63
13. Texas Toast 66
14. Aquarium 72
15. Dolphin Disruption 79
16. Hurricane Heroes 85

Meet the Jackson Family!

Leela

Jaden

Lucky

Lamar (Dad)

Jaya (Mom)

Welcome to Texas

"I win!" Leela Jackson cheered as she tossed a handful of cards onto the small kitchen table. "Beat you again. Six games in a row!"

Her younger brother, Jaden, crossed his arms. "No fair," he said. "You cheated."

"Did not! I'm just better at memory games than you," Leela said.

"I have a good memory," Jaden insisted.

"Can you *remember* to put your stinky socks in the laundry bin?" Leela crinkled her nose.

"Hey! My socks aren't stinky!" Jaden argued.

"Yeah, they are—" Leela disagreed.

"Kiddos," Mom started, "I know it's been a long trip, but we are getting close to the community shelter. We need to focus our energy on helping the people in Texas." Mom checked the messages on her phone.

When Mom's phone rang, it meant DISASTER!

When the phone rang, the Jackson family packed up their recreational vehicle, or RV, to help families during a natural disaster.

Everyone had an important role.

Mom was a famous journalist who took pictures and wrote news articles.

Dad was an award-winning doctor who helped people all over the world.

Jaden and Leela saved animals in danger.

Their German shepherd, Lucky, helped, too . . . when she wasn't napping.

For the past two days, they had been driving from northern California to southern Texas, where a hurricane was heading for the coast.

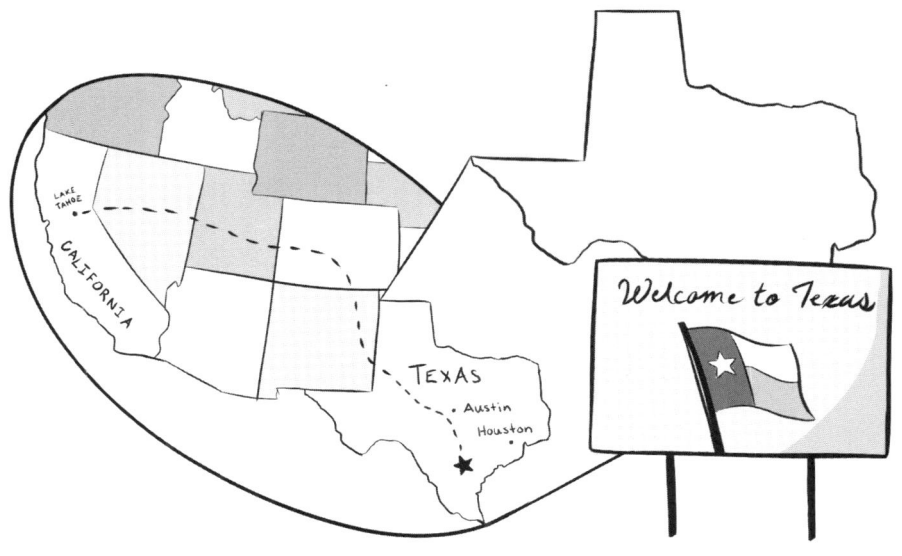

"Jacksons, welcome to the great state of Texas!" Dad announced as the RV drove past a large green sign.

Leela looked out the window. The ground was still low and flat, carpeted in bright green grass. Trees wrapped in leaves lined the sides of the road. It was the opposite of the black, burned land that had covered northern California at their last stop.

"I hope we get to taste some real Tex-Mex food!" Jaden said.

"We just had lunch," Leela reminded him. "Are you *always* hungry?"

"I hope I can get some good pictures," Mom said, adjusting her camera lens. "It's important that people see how natural disasters and climate change are affecting the planet."

Dad nodded. "I hope I have enough medical supplies to help anyone injured by the hurricane."

"What animals will we help in Texas?" Jaden wondered. "In just a week, we helped baby goats, a turtle, and I almost rescued a baby bear!"

Lucky barked. WOOF!

"Don't forget the deer," Leela said as she opened up her Disaster Squad Kit to make sure everything was inside. Every member of the Jackson family had their own kit.

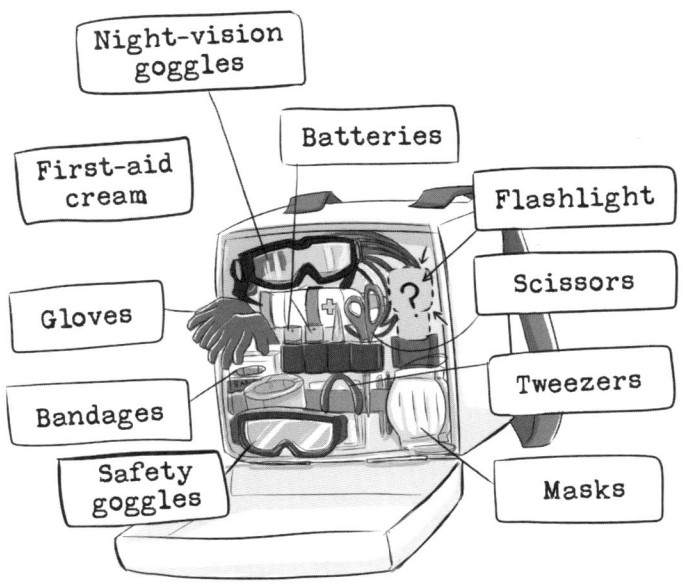

"Hey! Where's my flashlight?" Leela asked.

Jaden opened his kit. "Mine is missing, too," he said.

"I was wondering when you two would notice," Mom said. She turned and handed Jaden and Leela two small boxes. "Dad and I are so proud of how you helped during the wildfires in California. We got you these."

Jaden ripped the box open. He held up a blue flashlight. "A new flashlight! Cool!"

"They have rechargeable batteries," Leela added as she put her new purple flashlight into her kit.

Mom nodded. "Rechargeable batteries are better for the environment than regular batteries."

"Keep them charged," Dad instructed. "That's our turn up ahead. We are almost there—"

THUD!

2
Flat Tire

"What was that noise?" Jaden asked.

Jaden and Leela felt their seatbelts tighten as Dad held the steering wheel steady. They heard the noise again. It was coming from under the RV.

THUD THUD THUD.

"Did we hit something?" Leela frowned.

"It's just a flat tire," Dad said as he slowly and safely pulled off the main road.

Leela fastened Lucky's leash to her collar and held tight.

The Jackson family climbed out of the RV.

Dad opened a storage compartment. Inside was a spare tire, a toolbox, tire chocks, and a ramp jack. The ramp jack was a small platform that would help to hold the RV in place.

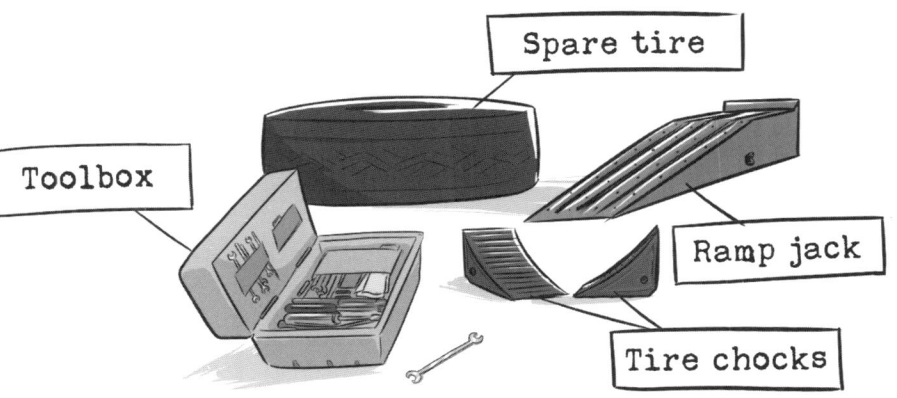

Dad placed the ramp jack in front of the RV's front right tire. Then he stood to the side.

Mom climbed into the driver's seat and slowly drove onto the ramp. Dad used tire chocks to secure the RV. Jaden handed Dad the toolbox as Mom turned off the RV and came outside to help.

As the tinkering sounds of wrenches on bolts echoed into the air, clouds began to cover the warm afternoon sun.

"I've got a joke," Dad started. "How many people does it take to fix a tire?"

Jaden groaned.

"Not another joke!" Leela shook her head.

"It's a good one!" Dad shrugged as he removed the flat tire and laid it on the ground. Mom held the new tire in place as Dad used a wrench to screw in the bolts.

"This is taking forever," Jaden grumbled, walking toward a pile of rocks. "I'm going to go explore."

"Jaden!" Leela exclaimed. "Come back!"

"Why?" Jaden frowned.

"Watch out!" Leela shouted. "There's a *snake*!"

Rattlesnake!

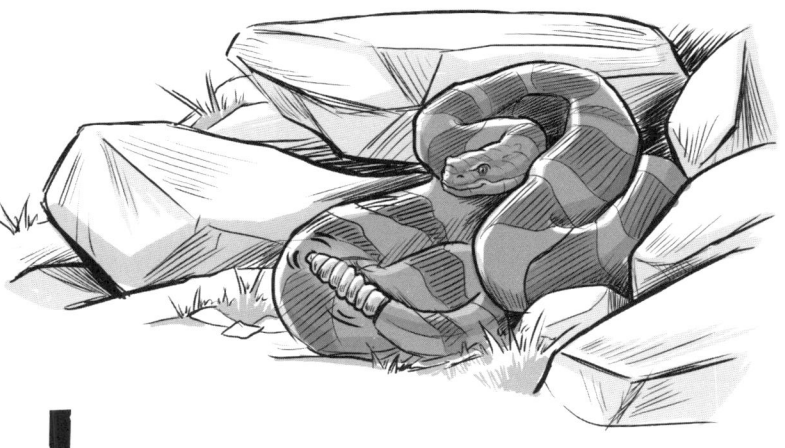

Leela pointed to a large brown snake curled up next to the rock pile.

The snake was camouflaged against the rocks. Its scales glistened in the afternoon sun. The tip of its tail had small thick rings that looked like a rattle.

TRRRRRRRR!

"Rattlesnake!" Jaden gasped.

Lucky barked. WOOF!

Leela held tightly on to Lucky's leash.

"There are more than ten species of rattlesnakes in this area," Mom said, walking over to them. "Be careful where you step."

"Should we move it off to the side?" Leela asked, remembering the turtle they helped across the road in California.

Mom shook her head. "No. Never touch a rattlesnake in the wild. They are very aggressive. Their bite is poisonous. Your aunt Maya often finds rattlesnakes in her backyard in Arizona. She calls a trained professional who captures the snakes and puts them safely back into the wild."

As they watched, the rattlesnake uncurled its body and slithered behind the rocks.

"Done!" Dad exclaimed proudly as he fixed the last bolt into the tire.

Mom checked her phone. "We should get going. We're already behind schedule."

Dad rolled the flat tire to the back of the RV.

Jaden bent down to help pack up the tools. "Hey! Who's spitting on me?" he asked.

"No one," Leela said, pointing up to the sky. Thick, dark clouds had quickly formed above them. Drops of rain splattered onto their foreheads and cheeks. The wind gusted faster, swirling Leela's long black hair around her shoulders.

"It was dry just a minute ago, and now rain. The storm is getting close!" Mom said, picking up the ramp jack.

"Can rattlesnakes swim?" Leela asked, looking worried.

Mom nodded. "Yes, and this is their natural habitat. They know how to survive the storm."

"It's only a few raindrops," Jaden said as he tilted his head back and opened his mouth to try to drink the rain.

BOOM! BOOM!

"Thunder!" Mom exclaimed, "Everyone get into the RV, now!"

The gentle raindrops suddenly grew bigger and began falling faster as they ran inside.

"Buckle up, everyone," Dad said, turning on the headlights and windshield wipers. Jaden and Leela buckled their seatbelts. Lucky huddled by Leela's feet.

"It's just a thunderstorm," Leela said quietly.

"This isn't just any thunderstorm," Mom added, looking out the window. "This . . . is the hurricane."

4
Hurricane Season

"We're *in* the hurricane?" Jaden asked.

Rain splattered against the windows.

The SWOOSH SWOOSH SWOOSH sound of the wipers grew louder as Dad steered the RV onto the road.

Even though it was warm inside the RV, Leela shivered as rain coated the windows.

Lucky whimpered.

"We aren't in the *actual* hurricane, Jaden," Mom replied. "We are in the beginning of the storm. It always rains before the hurricane travels inland after forming over the ocean."

"Hurricane season is definitely here," Dad added.

"There's a fire season *and* a hurricane season?" Jaden asked in disbelief. He remembered what Fire Chief Fran told them about wildfires in California and how there was a fire season every year.

Mom nodded. "Hurricane season in Texas usually starts in June and continues through November."

Jaden and Leela pulled open their tablets to research more information.

"Whoa," Jaden said. "Hurricanes are tropical storms that start in the water and come onto land. They can cause damage over one hundred miles from the coast." Jaden looked up from his tablet. "That's why it's raining here, even though we aren't near the ocean!"

"Scientists also say that there can be a hurricane watch or a hurricane warning," Leela added.

"What's the difference?" Jaden asked.

"A watch means a hurricane *might* happen. A warning means a hurricane is *definitely* going to happen." Leela paused, looking out at the storm.

Jaden pressed his face against the window. "I can't see a thing!" he said.

BAM! A small branch slammed against the RV window.

Jaden jerked back in his seat. "Did you see that?" he asked, eyes wide open.

Leela nodded and pointed back to her tablet. "When there's a hurricane, the winds can be up to 150 miles per hour," she read. "That's enough speed to pick up a car and throw it into a lake."

Ahead of them, bright red emergency lights flashed through the rain-covered windshield. A car was parked on the side of the road with its hood propped open.

"Oh no!" Mom said, pointing ahead. "Someone needs help!"

Tabby Cat

"**M**om and I are going to go help!" Dad said as he slowly pulled the RV behind the parked car. Mom and Dad put their rain gear on and ran outside.

Jaden and Leela stood up. They looked through the front window as the windshield wipers moved quickly from left to right.

SWOOSH SWOOSH SWOOSH.

Through the rain, they saw a young man standing outside his car, peering under the hood. He turned to talk to Mom and Dad as they ran up.

Dad helped push the car hood shut. Mom opened the passenger door and helped a younger girl get out. Together, everyone ran toward the RV.

The door of the RV slammed open and four people burst in!

Everyone was soaked.

Leela noticed the girl had a blanket wrapped carefully in her arms.

"Thank you for helping us," the young man said. "My name is Eric and this is my little sister, Olivia."

The Jacksons introduced themselves. Jaden handed out towels. Leela passed out water bottles.

Lucky barked. WOOF!

"What's wrong?" Leela asked, patting Lucky's head.

Olivia slowly opened the blanket in her arms, revealing what was inside.

"You have a cat!" Jaden said excitedly.

Olivia nodded. "He's a tabby. We had just adopted him at the animal shelter and were heading home. But then our car engine stopped working."

"We are going to the community shelter," Mom said. "Do you want to stay there until the storm ends?"

Eric nodded, holding up his phone. "I can call our dad to let him know. We'll have to come back for the car when it's safe."

The tabby cat shivered in Olivia's arms. It stuck a paw out of the wet blanket.

"It started raining as we walked out of the shelter," Olivia said. "He got drenched."

Leela took a small dry towel and handed it to Olivia. Olivia dried the cat's wet fur.

"What's your cat's name?" Jaden asked.

"We haven't named him yet," Olivia replied, setting the cat down next to her on the sofa.

Leela poured water into a small dish and left it next to the cat.

As they all sat down and buckled up, the cat slowly untangled himself from the towel and started to drink the water.

"He's thirsty!" Leela smiled.

Dad drove slowly in the rain, following the signs directing them to the community shelter.

Finally, Dad pulled into a large parking lot and parked the RV.

"Disaster Squad," Mom said. "We're here."

6
Community Shelter

Rain pattered loudly on the roof of the RV. Jaden and Leela sat up in their seats. They tried to to see through the heavy rain.

Mom handed out raincoats and rain boots. "Put these on, quickly!"

As the kids pulled on their rain gear, Mom tucked her camera into her coat and Dad grabbed his medical kit.

"Stay close," Dad said, holding open the door of the RV. Olivia ran ahead with the cat into the shelter. Eric, Mom, and Jaden followed.

"Come on, Lucky!" Leela said, grabbing her new flashlight and holding Lucky's leash tightly in her hand. Dad closed the RV door and ran behind Leela. Water splashed onto Leela's boots as she ran into the building.

Inside, Jaden and Leela stopped beside Olivia and Eric. They pulled off their hoods and looked around. The building was large and made of concrete.

On one side of the shelter, people were cramped into groups. Some were seated at round tables eating sandwiches. There were cots lined up in rows. Children were reading books or sleeping.

"Look!" Jaden said, pointing to the other side of the shelter. "They are building emergency kits! Just like the ones we helped make for the wildfires!"

Leela stood beside Olivia and scratched the tabby cat behind his ears. The cat purred.

"Thanks again," Eric said to the Jackson family as he gave Jaden a fist bump. "We're going to stay here until the hurricane passes through."

The Jackson family headed to the long tables, toward a woman dressed in gray pants and a button-down shirt.

"Jaden, Leela," Mom said, "I would like you to meet Mayor García."

"¿Cómo estás?" Mayor García extended her hand to Leela and Jaden, "How are you?"

"Hi." Leela smiled, shaking the mayor's hand. "It's nice to meet you."

Lucky wagged her tail.

"This shelter is huge," Mom said, looking around.

Mayor García nodded. "Sí, we built this shelter a few years ago. It is a place for people to stay safe during a hurricane or tornado. This is one of ten shelters in the area. It's the biggest one."

Jaden looked over at some firefighters standing by a table. "Why are firefighters here when there aren't any fires?"

"Buena pregunta," Mayor García said. "That's a great question. Hurricanes have strong winds that can knock down power lines. If those power lines catch fire, it can cause damage inside and outside of a building. The firefighters are prepared to respond."

"It would be so dark in here with no power," Leela pointed out.

"I know what would help!" Jaden said, running toward a large red door near the back of the shelter. "I want to get something from the RV!"

As Jaden grabbed the door handle, Mayor García ran after him shouting, "Don't open that door!"

7

Dos and Don'ts

"That's the emergency evacuation door! Don't open it, Jaden," Mayor García said.

Jaden turned around. "I just wanted to go get my new flashlight."

"We have a very important list of 'dos and don'ts' during a hurricane," Mayor García said. She pointed to a large sign on the shelter wall where there were directions in both English and Spanish. Leela read the English dos aloud:

EMERGENCY DOS AND DON'TS

DO board up windows.
DO pack water and non-perishable foods.
DO keep a first-aid kit and
charge cell phones.
DO check for fallen power lines.
DO use the main door to enter and exit.
DO have flashlights and extra batteries.

"My turn!" Jaden said. He read the English don'ts aloud.

DON'T stand near windows.
DON'T ignore the smell of gas.
DON'T touch electrical wires.
DON'T ignore evacuation orders and
think you are safe!
DON'T use the emergency evacuation
door unless instructed.

"The emergency evacuation door can only be opened when you're told to do so. You can go through the main doors if you need to go outside," Mayor García explained.

Leela put her hand on Jaden's shoulder. "I brought my flashlight. We can share."

Two firefighters walked over to Mayor García. They spoke quietly as Mom took pictures of them.

The Jacksons stood nearby as Mayor García made an announcement over the intercom. "Por favor, everyone stay calm. Please remember not to panic and always ask for help . . . because Hurricane Connor is here."

8
Hurricane Connor

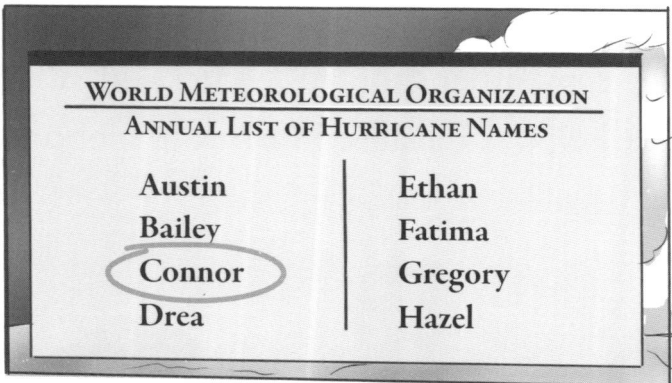

"The hurricane is named Connor?" Jaden asked.

"Meteorologists use the names to track the storms," Leela explained. "They name hurricanes, tornadoes, and even cyclones!"

"The World Meteorological Organization has six lists of names," Mayor García added. "The list rotates every six years. There are also different names for hurricanes that form in the Atlantic Ocean and those in the Pacific."

"Can they name a hurricane after me?" Jaden asked.

Mayor García smiled. "The names are picked each previous year, in alphabetical order."

Dad sighed. "I remember the damage from Hurricane Andrew in 1992. It ripped off your Uncle Matt's roof in Miami, Florida."

"And Hurricane Katrina in 2005 flooded buildings and schools in New Orleans, Louisiana . . ." Mom's voice trailed off.

Mayor García nodded. "In 2017, Hurricane Harvey was one of the most devastating hurricanes to hit South Texas. Many people are still struggling to repair the damage to their homes."

Mayor García pulled out a stack of pamphlets. She handed one to Jaden and one to Leela. "We have been working with local government to help share information.

There are five categories of hurricanes." She pointed to the middle of the pamphlet. "Connor is a Category 2 hurricane. Thankfully, it's not one of the biggest."

"How can we help?" Mom asked.

Mayor García checked a message on her phone. "We have a smaller shelter about five miles from here. They need help boarding up windows. Even though shelters are built to withstand strong winds, the boards provide extra protection."

"But don't you need help making the emergency kits?" Leela asked, looking over at the long tables.

"Gracias. Thank you, but we have enough people helping in here. The other shelter doesn't have as many resources," Mayor García replied.

Mom shook Mayor García's hand and nodded. "We'll stay in touch. Jackson family, let's go!"

As the Jackson family headed to the main door of the building, the lights inside the shelter started to blink–

CRACK FIZZ CRACK!

Lucky barked. WOOF!

Mom took Lucky's leash from Leela. Leela reached out and held Mom's free hand tightly.

Jaden looked up at the white lights that lined the ceiling. Each row started to flicker. Then, suddenly, all of the lights in the shelter went out.

It was a blackout!

9
Shadow Puppet Show

"**O**h no!" Jaden gasped. "The power is out!"

"Do not worry, mis amigos," Mayor García said loudly. "It's common for power outages to happen during a hurricane. The shelter's generator will start soon. The generator is a backup power source for our building."

Inside the shelter, people turned on flashlights from their emergency kits.

"I'm scared," someone said.

Jaden turned toward the voice. He saw a little boy sitting on the floor. His mom was holding his hand.

"Hi," Jaden said, crouching down next to them. "My name is Jaden. What's yours?"

The little boy looked at his mom, then back to Jaden.

"Luis," he said shyly.

"Don't worry," Leela said. "Sometimes the power and lights go out during big storms."

"I don't like the dark, either," Jaden said. "Want to do something fun?"

Luis nodded.

"Let's make shadow puppets!" Jaden suggested.

"We can use my flashlight!" Leela added.

As Leela shone her flashlight at the dark wall, Jaden locked his thumbs together and lifted out his other fingers, flapping them across the light.

"Birdie!" Luis cheered.

Jaden moved to the other side of the light and put his hand in a fist, then pushed up his index finger and middle finger. He bounced his hand across the light as he curled the tips of his fingers up and down.

"Bunny!" said another voice behind him. Jaden turned to see a small crowd of children were sitting and watching. He smiled.

"Alligator!"

"Dinosaur!"

Voices called out through the dark as Jaden and Leela continued their shadow puppet show.

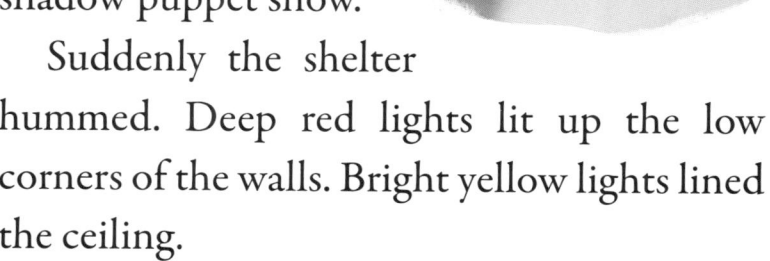

Suddenly the shelter hummed. Deep red lights lit up the low corners of the walls. Bright yellow lights lined the ceiling.

The generator had turned the lights back on! Everyone cheered. Leela saw that Eric and Olivia had been watching the shadow puppet show.

"Thanks for helping my son feel better," Luis's mom said to Jaden.

"Great show," Olivia added.

"That was wonderful," Mom said. "You both helped make a lot of little kids feel safe."

"Jackson family!" Dad shouted over the noise. "It's time to go to the smaller shelter. Come on!"

10
Flood!

"**H**urry up!" Dad called out. "We need to get to the other shelter before the storm picks up speed."

The Jacksons waved goodbye to Eric, Olivia, and Mayor García before heading back into the storm.

Rain soaked the Jackson family as they ran into the RV. Lucky barked loudly as they all jumped inside.

Dad started the RV as Mom passed out towels. Outside, the wind howled and the streets were covered in shallow water. The RV swayed gently from side to side as Dad steadied the steering wheel and started to drive away.

"Look!" Leela pointed. A small log floated in deeper water on the edge of the road. Trees bent and swayed from side to side. Their branches waved in the wind.

"This isn't safe," Dad started. "We need to get off the roads before the water gets too deep."

"The shelter is just ahead!" Mom said.

Around them, cars had pulled over. People were getting out of their cars and running toward the shelter.

Dad tried to steer the RV up a small hill and into the parking lot of the shelter, but the RV wouldn't move.

Dad tried to reverse the RV, but the water levels were getting higher.

"We're stuck!" Leela worried.

"We will have to run into the shelter, too," Dad said. He put the RV in park. The Jackson family grabbed their gear and jumped out of the RV. They dashed to the shelter. Water fell heavily around them as they ran up the hill.

"Be careful!" Mom said, holding tightly on to Lucky's leash.

"It's pouring! I can't see!" Jaden cried as he slipped and fell into the water.

Dad grabbed Jaden's arm and helped him up. He kept a firm hold on Jaden's arm, guiding him up the hill. Rain drenched the Jackson family as they finally made it to the shelter.

As Leela held the shelter door open for her family, she glanced at the road below them.

A wave of water filled the streets, spilling onto the sidewalks and reaching the bottom of the bushes. At the bottom of the hill, Leela saw a small, empty car. It started to bob up and down in the water.

Leela gasped and slammed the door, shutting them inside.

Board Up

"The roads are flooded!" Leela said as she joined her family inside the shelter. "We got here just in time!"

Mom put her arm around Leela's shoulders. "We are safe now and can wait out the storm in here. Roads often flood during a hurricane. The best place to be is indoors."

Jaden and Leela looked around the community shelter. It was smaller than the shelter they came from and was packed with people sitting side by side.

"Hola!" someone greeted them.

Everyone turned to see a man with brown hair walking toward them. He was followed by a young girl leading a large dog on a leash.

"Hello!" Dad said, extending his hand. "I'm Lamar Jackson, and this is my wife, Jaya, and our children."

"Welcome! Thank you for coming to help. My name is Marcos Martinez and this is my daughter, Maria," Marcos said, motioning to the girl.

Leela smiled. "My name is Leela! You have a German shepherd, too!"

"His name is Rocky," Maria said. "He's a rescue."

"Can I pet him?" Jaden asked.

Maria nodded.

Jaden scratched Rocky behind his ear. Rocky wagged his tail.

"What is your German shepherd's name?" Maria asked, excited.

"Her name is Lucky," Leela said.

Lucky moved close to Rocky and sniffed his face. Rocky licked Lucky's nose.

"I manage this shelter," Marcos told the Jackson family. "We never imagined we would need to board up windows so soon."

Dad nodded. "What can we do to help?"

Marcos pointed to a far corner of the shelter. "We need to finish boarding up the windows at the back before it gets dark."

"Rocky and I can watch Lucky while you work," Maria said. Mom handed her Lucky's leash. Then Dad and Mom each grabbed two boards. Jaden and Leela each carried a small bucket of nails and hammers. Dad and Jaden worked on the windows at one end of the wall while Mom and Leela started on the other end.

"Let's see who gets to the middle first!" Jaden shouted across the shelter.

Leela shook her head. "It's not a race!" she called back.

Mom held a board against the wall with one hand. Leela held out a nail and Mom hammered it into the board.

The sound of many hammers hitting nails echoed through the shelter.

BAM! BAM! BAM!

"Leela, hand me one more nail," Mom said as she finished hammering in a second board.

"We're faster!" Jaden called, handing Dad another nail.

BAM! BAM! BAM!

"Can I try to use the hammer?" Leela asked Mom.

Mom nodded as she held the board in place. "Hold the nail steady."

BAM! BAM! BAM!

"Great job!" Mom said.

"Thanks." Leela smiled.

Leela worked with Mom and hammered in two more boards.

"I'm going to take a few more photos. Can you finish up?" Mom asked.

Leela nodded.

"Let me help!" Jaden jogged over. "Dad and I are done." He reached for the hammer.

"Jaden, Mom told me to finish." Leela said, yanking the hammer back. It slipped out of her hand, falling and landing heavily on her foot.

Leela grabbed her foot as she crumbled to the floor. "OW!"

WHAM!

12
Hail!

"Leela!" Dad ran toward her.

Dad quickly opened his medical kit. "Let me look at your foot."

Jaden crouched down next to Leela and put an arm around her shoulders. "Sorry, Leela. I was just trying to help."

"I know." Leela sighed.

Dad removed Leela's shoe and checked her foot. "It looks like it's just a bruise," he said. He opened his medical kit and took out an instant ice pack. He cracked the ice pack in half to activate the cold. Then, he placed it on Leela's foot to stop the swelling.

"The rain is getting heavier," Marcos said, walking over with Mom. "It's probably best if your family stays here for a while."

The boards on the windows started shaking as the pounding of rain rattled the rooftop.

THUMP THUMP THUMP.

Leela looked around and saw families huddled together. Children were lying down on the floor, wrapped in blankets and cuddled in sleeping bags. Someone started crying. People were whispering.

Dad looked at Mom. "The storm is getting worse," he said.

Mom nodded. "Jackson family," she said softly. "Let's get settled in these sleeping bags. We are staying in the shelter tonight."

Jaden and Leela tucked into the sleeping bags and soon fell asleep with Lucky curled between them. They all wondered if the hurricane would ever end.

13
Texas Toast

Jaden woke to something wet and soggy on his face.

SLURP!

He opened his eyes to see Lucky standing over him, her long tongue dangling close to his face.

"Lucky!" Jaden laughed as he hugged her. Lucky wagged her tail.

Jaden rubbed his eyes and sat up. He turned around to see his family sitting at a table. Dad was packing his medical supplies. Leela was eating a granola bar. Mom was looking at the pictures on her camera.

Jaden and Lucky walked over to where the others were sitting.

"About time." Leela laughed. "I sent Lucky to wake you up!"

"Is the hurricane gone?" Jaden asked.

"Not yet," Mom shook her head. "But the worst of the storm is over. It lasted about eight hours. The focus now is on fixing the damage and helping people get home safely."

Around the shelter, families were sitting at tables or gathered together on the floor. They were eating bars and drinking juice that volunteers were passing out.

"Can we drive in the RV?" Leela asked, remembering the car she saw bobbing in the flooded street.

"Yes," Dad said. "We will drive it to higher ground now that the flooding has started to clear up."

"Buenos días!" Maria said as she walked over to the Jackson family. She handed out large slices of toast.

"Good morning, Maria," Mom replied.

"When my papi is at the shelter, I love to make Texas toast for everyone." Maria smiled.

Jaden and Leela each took a bite of the thick, crunchy bread.

"YUM!" Jaden said. "This is the best toast ever. Is it really from Texas?"

Maria laughed. "It's just extra-thick toast. I have never been anywhere but Texas. I don't know if they have it in other places."

"It's delicious," Dad said.

"Thank you for the toast, Maria!" Mom said. "You kids stay here. Dad and I need to go check in with Marcos." Mom and Dad stood up and walked toward the front of the shelter where Maria's father was unpacking water bottles.

"Why haven't you left Texas?" Leela asked. Maria sat down at the table.

"It's very expensive to travel, and we have to take care of my abuela, who is very old and sick. Papi says it's important we help the people in our community before we help ourselves." Maria paused. "One day I want to travel the world and share my recipes."

Jaden took another bite of toast. "I want your toast recipe!" he exclaimed.

"I'll tell it to you!" Maria smiled. "Then you can take the recipe and add whatever you want. Then it becomes your own special toast."

As Jaden finished writing down the recipe, Mom and Dad ran over.

"Kiddos, we have to go. I just got a call," Mom said, looking worried. "There's a dolphin trainer at the aquarium who needs medical attention. And a dolphin calf has gone missing!"

14
Aquarium

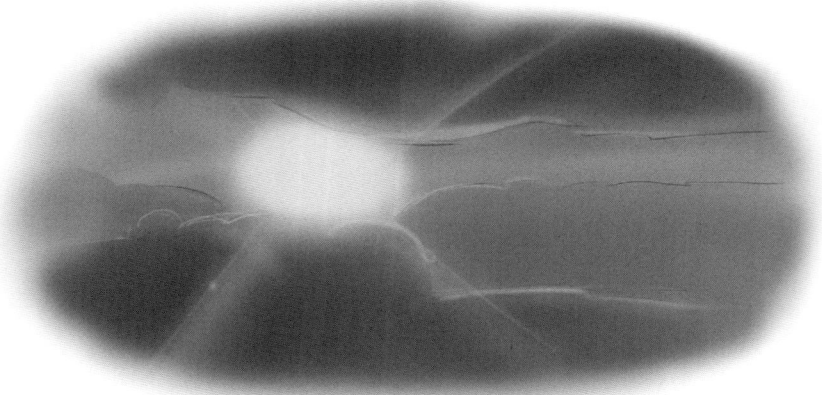

"**A** baby dolphin has gone missing!" Leela repeated as they rushed to the RV. They waved goodbye to Marcos and Maria, who stood at the shelter door.

Mom drove the RV toward the aquarium as Dad passed out more snacks. Jaden looked out the window. The heavy rains that had battered the top of the shelter had turned into a light drizzle.

The street flooding had gone down. The thick clouds that had covered the sky were slowly parting. A hint of a bright blue sky peeked through. As they drove, Jaden and Leela looked out the window. They saw trees broken and fallen across the road, windows smashed on homes without boards, and a telephone pole lying on the ground.

About twenty minutes later, the RV pulled up to the aquarium. Two people dressed in tight black wetsuits greeted the Jacksons outside.

"Thank you for coming. I'm Andrea and this is our other lead trainer, Paola," one of the trainers said.

"Happy to help," Dad said. "Can you tell us what happened?"

"When the storm ended, we were finally able to open the gate to the outside pen for the dolphin calves to swim," Paola said.

"The feeding dock was still wet," Andrea explained. "Another trainer, Sofia, slipped while trying to feed the dolphin calves and hurt her arm on a metal pole. Ambulances are backed up because of the hurricane. That's why we called you!"

Dad held up his medical kit and followed Andrea inside the aquarium.

"What about the dolphin calf?" Leela asked. "How did it go missing? We'd like to help find it!"

"When we opened the first gate, one of the dolphins somehow escaped past the barrier." Paola gestured as everyone followed her around the back of the aquarium. "We think the second gate jammed because of the hurricane. That gate opens into the bay." Paola pointed toward the bay down below.

WOOF! WOOF! Lucky pulled away from Leela's grasp and ran down a steep hill.

"Lucky!" Leela shouted, running after her. Jaden and Mom followed closely behind.

Lucky didn't stop. She ran faster and faster to the beach.

Suddenly, Lucky stopped at the edge of the water, sniffing and circling something small and dark that lay on the sand.

It was the baby dolphin!

15
Dolphin Disruption

"**W**e found the missing dolphin!" Jaden gasped as Leela took hold of Lucky's leash.

Lying on the sand was a baby dolphin. Its eyes were closed.

"Is it hurt?" Leela asked.

Paola looked carefully before shaking her head no. "After escaping from the aquarium, she must have gotten stranded. We need to get her back to the aquarium so we can help her recover."

Leela knelt down and rubbed Lucky's ears. "Good job, girl!" she said.

Lucky barked. WOOF!

"Take handfuls of water and pour them over the dolphin," Paola instructed. "The water will help keep her cool and wet! But don't pour water into the blowhole—that's where the dolphin breathes air."

"I'll get the buckets the farmer gave us during the dust storm!" Leela said as she quickly ran to the RV and brought back five buckets. Paola ran back to the aquarium to get a stretcher.

"Keep pouring, kiddos," Mom said.

Jaden and Leela poured more water over the dolphin calf.

The dolphin wriggled in the sand and opened her eyes.

Paola ran toward the beach with the stretcher. Mom, Jaden, and Leela helped to slowly lift the calf onto the stretcher, rushing her back inside the aquarium.

"Great work!" Paola said once the calf was safely in her tank with her family. The calf dove into the water and leaped out, swimming alongside her mom and sibling.

Jaden and Leela cheered! "Hooray!"

"Dolphins born in captivity don't know how to survive in the wild," Paola explained. "We help teach them how to survive in the wild so they can be released safely. This one wasn't ready because she is too young."

The Jacksons smiled as they watched the calves and their mother swim.

Once the dolphins were settled and Dad had finished putting Sofia's arm in a sling, the Jacksons climbed into the RV. It was time to head back to the main shelter and check on their new friends.

16
Hurricane Heroes

"You're back!" Eric said. He and Olivia walked over to the Jackson family as they got out of the RV at the main shelter.

Olivia was holding their cat.

Leela rubbed the cat's paw. "Does he have a name yet?"

Olivia nodded. "We decided to name him Jackson, after your family."

"You guys saved us from being stranded in the hurricane. Now we will always remember your family," Eric added.

"That's so thoughtful," Mom said, smiling.

"I hope you come back to visit," Olivia said.

"Sí! We will definitely call the Disaster Squad again!" Mayor García said as she walked over to the Jacksons. "You are hurricane heroes!" She handed Jaden and Leela each a small badge.

"Cool!" Jaden said as he pinned the badge to his shirt.

"And for Lucky," Mayor García said, "I have a special pin for your collar."

Lucky sat up straight and wagged her tail.

The Jackson family waved goodbye to their new friends. Then they climbed into the RV to clean up and rest.

"Whew!" Dad said as he sat on the sofa. "That was one tough disaster."

"I'm glad we are all safe. Mayor García said that they will be receiving extra supplies from the state of Texas to start clearing the damaged areas," Mom added. "Who's hungry?"

"Me!" Jaden and Leela said at the same time. "Jinx! Double jinx. Triple jinx!"

"I'm going to make my own special Texas toast," Jaden said, opening a loaf of bread.

Jaden followed Maria's recipe and passed out slices of thick, buttery Texas toast.

"Yum!" Dad exclaimed as he crunched on the toast.

"This is good," Leela said, and winked at Jaden, "but not as good as Maria's."

Jaden stuck his tongue out at Leela.

Lucky curled up next to Leela's feet and fell asleep.

"I'm going to beat you at another game of cards." Leela laughed, pointing at Jaden.

"No way!" Jaden replied.

"I'm ready for a nice long nap," Dad said.

Suddenly, Mom's phone rang.

Everyone was quiet. Mom answered the phone and walked to the back of the RV. Jaden and Leela watched as she frowned and shook her head. When Mom nodded, they nodded. When she shook her head, they shook their heads.

"Okay, Ma, talk to you soon," Mom said as she hung up the phone. She walked back to the table.

"Was that Gramma?" Leela asked.

Mom nodded. "I have good news and bad news," she said. "Which do you want to hear first?"

"Good news!" Jaden said quickly.

Mom smiled. "The good news is that we get to see Gramma and visit her at her home in Minnesota."

"Gramma!" Leela cheered.

"What's the bad news?" Dad asked.

"The bad news," Mom said as she frowned, "is that the entire community is preparing . . . for a disaster!"

About the Creators

Rekha S. Rajan is the author of several children's books including *Amazing Landmarks*, the This Is Music series, and *Can You Dance Like a Peacock?* She is a musician with a doctorate in education, and she works with educators nationwide to bring STEAM learning to the classroom. She spent her childhood visiting Miami, Florida, where she saw the damage that hurricanes caused and how communities came together to help. She lives in Chicago with her husband, three children, a lot of animals, and their German shepherd named Lucky.

Courtney Lovett is the illustrator of several children's books, including *Join the Club, Maggie Diaz*; *Santa's Gotta Go*; and *Basketball Dreams*, written by NBA all-star Chris Paul. She received her BFA in illustration and animation from UMBC. Utilizing both skill sets, she is driven to create stories that spark imagination and wonder in children. Today, she lives in her hometown in Maryland, where she illustrates books and teaches at a local art studio.

Hurricane Rescue
Questions & Activities

Look up the definition of a hurricane. Compare and contrast a hurricane, a cyclone, and a typhoon.

What things can you do to stay safe during a hurricane? How did Jaden and Leela help keep the community safe during the hurricane?

How do hurricanes get their names? What would you name a hurricane?

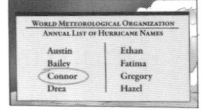

What animals did Leela and Jaden meet in this book? Which animal is your favorite?

Why was it dangerous for Jaden and Leela to approach the rattlesnake? What would you have done?

Leela and Jaden travel across the country in their RV. Draw and label a map of where they travel! What states do they visit? What states do they drive through on their way to Texas?

scholastic.com/branches